Mo...ce

In...rs

Vic Parker

C2 000 004 768024

www.raintreepublishers.co.uk
Visit our website to find out
more information about
Raintree books.

To order:
☎ Phone 0845 6044371
🖷 Fax +44 (0) 1865 312263
🖳 Email myorders@raintreepublishers.co.uk

Customers from outside the UK please telephone +44 1865 312262

Raintree is an imprint of Capstone Global Library Limited,
a company incorporated in England and Wales having its
registered office at 7 Pilgrim Street, London, EC4V 6LB –
Registered company number: 6695582

Edited by Nancy Dickmann and Laura Knowles
Designed by Victoria Allen
Picture research by Mica Brančić
Illustrations by HL Studios
Originated by Capstone Global Library Ltd
Printed and bound in China by CTPS

ISBN 978 1 406 23961 4 (hardback)
16 15 14 13 12
10 9 8 7 6 5 4 3 2 1

ISBN 978 1 406 23966 9 (paperback)
17 16 15 14 13
10 9 8 7 6 5 4 3 2 1

British Library Cataloguing in Publication Data
Parker, Victoria.
Inspiring others. -- (Making a difference)
302.1'4-dc23
A full catalogue record for this book is available from the
British Library.

Acknowledgements
The author and publisher are grateful to the following for
permission to reproduce copyright material: Adora Lily
Svitak pp. 27, 28, 29, 30; Corbis pp. 7 (© MM Productions), 13
(© Rubberball), 39 (Reuters/X01848/© Parth Sanyal), 41 (Condé
Nast/© WWD); Free The Children pp. 36, 37; Getty Images p. 31
(Ben Gabbe); Josh Schipp p. 40; Lutheran General Children's
Hospital pp. 9, 10, 12; Matt Lovett pp. 17, 19 bottom; Newark
Advertiser p. 15; Press Association Images p. 34 (AP/Tom
Hanson), 38 (The Canadian Press Images/Christian Lapid), 33
(Scanpix/Ylwa Yngvesson); Project Jatropha pp. 22, 24, 25;
Shutterstock pp. 19 top (© Christopher Parypa), 21 (© Steve
Estvanik), 23 (© Rufous); Superstock p. 4 (© Science Faction);
Tom Lochmüller p. 5.

Cover photograph of children reproduced with permission of
Corbis/cultura/© Moment.

Background design images supplied by Shutterstock/Toria/
ZeroTO/silver-john.

Every effort has been made to contact copyright holders
of material reproduced in this book. Any omissions will be
rectified in subsequent printings if notice is given to the
publisher.

Starting with a special skill

What are you particularly good at? Maybe it's writing, maths, singing, inventing, entertaining, or caring for others. Everyone is good at something. However, while many people just enjoy using their talents for fun, some people use their skills to inspire others, to give something back to the world and try to make it a better place.

Wacky Rymel has used his special talent to inspire young people living in an **underprivileged** area.

Kids who made a difference

In 2009, 16-year-old Wacky Rymel (real name Rymel Lawrence) entered a competition called Good for the Hood. Wacky lived in Hackney – a part of London filled with gangs, guns, and knife crime. He had an inspiring plan to get kids off the street by offering free dance classes. Wacky came first and won funding to get his idea off the ground.

Starting with a passion

Some people who inspire others begin with a **cause** that they believe in, rather than having a special talent. What issues are you enthusiastic about? Maybe you're passionate about protecting animals, or helping homeless people? Perhaps you're keen to get involved in fundraising for a local theatre or sports club? Find out which causes your friends, neighbours, and family are helping and see if you would like to join them.

How to inspire others

Inspirational people have several things in common: energy and enthusiasm, courage to try something difficult, and **determination** not to give up when the going gets tough. They also grab opportunities when they come along or make their own opportunities when they don't!

Top tips

If you want to achieve something inspirational, make a plan. Grab a pen and paper and write down where you are now, and where you want to be in a certain amount of time. Then set yourself small goals to reach along the way. Just focus on achieving one small goal at a time. They will add up to great things.

School gardens such as Project Sprout help young people learn more about the food they eat.

Kids who made a difference

In 2009, 13-year-old Sam Levin, from Massachusetts, USA, wanted to help the **environment**. He set up an **organic** garden at school, run by the students. It began supplying the school's cafeteria with fresh fruit and vegetables. Sam's effort inspired many others to get involved, from kindergarten pupils to local businesses. It inspired three other local schools to start a garden, as well as schools in Uganda and Senegal.

7

Abby Enck: inspiring others to help sick children

In North America, some children have fun and make a little pocket money by selling homemade lemonade on street stalls. Some young people give the money they make to charity. For instance, Sarah Connor of New York began selling lemonade when she was six. By the time she was eleven, she had set up an organization called Project Lemon Aid and made over US$6,000 for good causes. She was able to help the American Cancer Society, victims of Hurricane Katrina, and a local tree-planting scheme. However, few young people have inspired so many others to run their own lemonade stands as Abby Enck, from Illinois, USA.

Abby Enck lives in the city of Chicago, Illinois, USA.

A cheering inspiration

Abby Enck was born in 2002. Her younger brother was diagnosed with **cerebral palsy** when he was just one week old. This is a medical condition where part of a baby's brain does not grow as it should. It causes problems with the child's movement and **coordination**. Some people are affected only mildly, others more severely.

Abby's brother needed regular visits to the local hospital for treatment, and she always went along too. When Abby was seven, she noticed that many of the young patients in the waiting room enjoyed colouring, but most of the hospital's crayons were broken. Abby wanted to help, but how?

Abby's brother was treated at the Lutheran General Children's Hospital, Illinois, USA.

Abby inspires her family

Abby told her mum and dad that she wanted to set up a lemonade stand to raise money to buy crayons for the children at the hospital. Her parents were so impressed that they agreed to match however many crayons Abby could buy with the same number themselves. During the summer of 2009, Abby raised enough money for 18 boxes of crayons. Her parents matched this, making 36 boxes for the young patients. But Abby didn't want to stop there.

Abby came up with a catchy slogan for her lemonade-selling project: "When life gives you lemons, colour!" This is one of Abby's lemonade kits.

Abby inspires her friends

The next summer, Abby set her sights higher. She created lemonade kits made up of bottles of water with a packet of ingredients and a homemade label. She made a list of possible customers and emailed them information about her kits. Then Abby **recruited** her family and friends to sell kits too, for US$1 each. She organized their stands for them and in return they gave her some of their **profits**. In this way, Abby made enough money to buy nearly 1,000 more boxes of crayons. But her efforts had inspired even more people to get involved.

Top tips

Would you like to set up your own lemonade stand to raise money for a charity? First, think about how you could get the money for the ingredients you need. Maybe you could earn money by doing extra jobs around the house for cash, or perhaps you know a neighbour who would pay you to help with gardening. Always ask your parents first if you are allowed to do something like this. Or perhaps you could make greetings cards to sell to your family and friends. Find out about local school or community fairs where you might be able to sell lots of lemonade.

Ask an adult to help you make your own lemonade:
- Heat one cup of water with one cup of sugar in a saucepan, until the sugar dissolves.
- Put this into a jug in the fridge to cool. Then add the juice from 4 to 6 lemons and 4 cups of cold tap water (or sparkling water, if you like your lemonade fizzy), and stir.

Branching out

The local newspaper printed a story about Abby's efforts and suddenly businesses began to help her. Some companies agreed to sell lemonade kits for her, while others **donated** money. Their generosity was inspired by Abby's hard work and determination to help the young patients at the hospital.

Abby raised enough money to buy 1,009 boxes of crayons, 140 boxes of pens, and 125 boxes of coloured pencils. The hospital was amazed and delighted.

Abby Enck was ranked number one in a major website's list of Inspiring Acts in 2010.

In their own words

Mother Teresa, a Catholic nun who worked with the poor and the sick in India, once said, "We ourselves feel that what we are doing is just a drop in the ocean. But the ocean would be less because of that missing drop."

Abby's ambitions

Abby now has even greater plans. She has had the idea of selling microwave popcorn packages to raise money to buy DVDs for the young patients in the hospital. She also continues to inspire others – her Girl Scout troop has been **brainstorming** ways to help. "Everyone can make a difference," says Abby.

Hospitals often do not have enough money to buy items like DVDs for patients.

Top tips

If you would like to raise funds by having a tabletop sale, get other people to help. Ask your family and friends to donate things to sell and help you make a sign. Make sure you have an adult on the stand with you, as it is not safe to do this alone.

Matt Lovett: an inspiration for young entrepreneurs

For teenagers today, life may seem all doom and gloom. Many young people have little money to spend on things they enjoy, such as activities with friends, hobbies, and music. The press is filled with bad stories about how teenagers hang around on street corners, getting into trouble. Reports talk about how jobs will be hard for them to find in future.

However, Matt Lovett from Birmingham, UK should be an inspirational **role model** for young people. His story shows that if you have some get up and go, you can make your future bright.

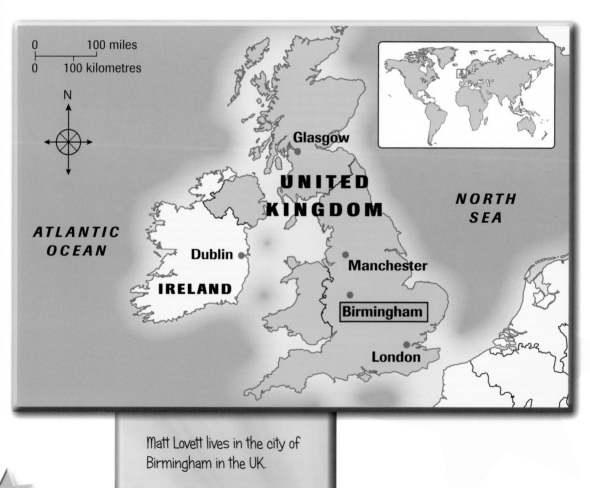

Matt Lovett lives in the city of Birmingham in the UK.

A schoolboy businessman

Born in 1991, Matt grew up watching his father run his own car sales business. Matt wanted to make his own money, too. At 13, he used his pocket money to buy sweets and sell them at school. The teachers there realized he had great ideas. They entered him into a project for young **entrepreneurs**, to learn business skills. Matt learned how to keep sales records, and about different ways of advertising products. Matt was determined to put the sweet sale profits to use in a bigger, better business idea.

Matt Lovett has been a businessman since school.

Top tips

The first step in starting any business is to develop a business plan. A business plan is a list or description of what you plan to do, how much it will cost, and how much you expect to make from your business. A business plan may also include information about your future customers, or plans on how to advertise to people.

A bright idea

Matt soon had an idea. He was a regular user of online cashback websites. These make money by charging companies to advertise their products and services, just as they do on television and radio and in magazines. Shoppers buy from the websites because they are offered cash back or rewards if they do. So this way, the companies make sales, the shoppers get bargains, and the cashback site makes money, too.

Matt thought that he could do a better job than the cashback sites were doing, so he set up his own. It did £30 of business on its first day, which was an exciting achievement. Even more exciting, by the time Matt was 14, the website was making over £1,000 a month.

In their own words
Matt Lovett's advice to other young entrepreneurs is: "It doesn't matter what your age is – what matters is how good your idea is."

Wow!

When Matt was 16, he set up another internet company, called WOW media. The company did so well that he left school to concentrate on it. WOW media worked in a similar way to Matt's first cashback company, but Matt developed several websites rather than just one. By the end of the year, after a lot of hard work, Matt had 20 websites, an office, and six staff, and was making £25,000 every month! WOW Media was valued to be worth £1,000,000. On top of all this, Matt was announced as the winner of a competition for Enterprising Young Brits run by the *Daily Mail* newspaper.

The Enterprising Young Brits competition was held to find the most promising young businessperson in Britain.

WOW media

Top tips

If you want to set up your own business, trying hard at many school subjects can be very helpful. It's important to be able to read well so you can do things such as checking over business agreements, to make sure no one is cheating you! If you can write clearly and stylishly, you will be able to communicate well with your customers and other business people. Maths skills will help you keep track of how much money you are making – or losing! Technology and business studies courses can teach you special skills to help your company beat the competition. And language skills can help you expand your business to a worldwide scale!

Inspiring others

After his success, Matt wanted to give something back. He decided to work to inspire other young people who might have an instinct for business. He began a new company called Your Brand, which helps other people to set up their own cashback websites. He also started taking on **apprentices**, to train young people and encourage others to achieve business success.

Matt meets his inspiration

In 2011, Matt won a national business competition for young people that was run by the company Virgin. The competition's prize was to meet the owner of Virgin, the billionaire businessman Richard Branson. For Matt, this was a dream come true.

By 2011, WOW Media was operating in five countries with over 250,000 members. Matt's success has made him money, but it has also enabled him to create jobs. This helps the economy, as does training apprentices. Matt proves that if you are a young person with good ideas and a brain for business, it is possible to compete in an adult world and win.

In their own words

The billionaire businessman Richard Branson wants more young people to come up with good new business ideas: "If you have a good entrepreneurial idea, you should go for it ... It's important we encourage and invest in new business ventures."

Kids who made a difference

Richard Branson was born in Surrey, England, in 1950. He left school aged 16 and set up a magazine for young people called *Student*. By the age of 22 he had opened a mail-order record delivery company, a record shop, a recording studio, and a record label, Virgin. He later set up an airline and other companies, and became one of the richest businessmen in the world.

The entrepreneur Richard Branson is Matt Lovett's all-time hero.

Apoorva and Adarsha: working for a better world

In 2007, sister and brother Apoorva Rangan and Adarsha Shivakumar were 13 and 14 years old. They lived in Oakland, California, USA, but every year they went to spend the summer with their grandparents on their family farm in Karnataka, India. All around the farm there were villages where the people were extremely poor. Most of the villagers made a living by growing tobacco. However, they had to put their tobacco plants through a special drying process before they could sell their harvest. This meant spending most of their money on buying firewood to make fires for the drying. The villagers had very little money left over to buy food and clothes.

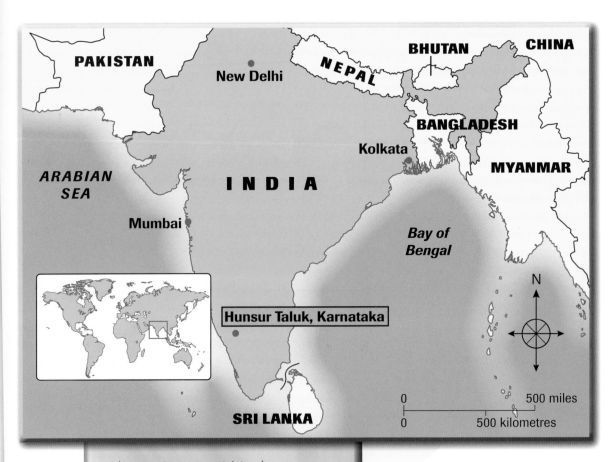

Apoorva Rangan and Adarsha Shivakumar live part of the year in the USA and part of the year in India.

Inspired by poverty

Every summer, Apoorva and Adarsha asked friends and family to donate clothes. They took the clothes to India and gave them out to the very poor village children. These children often wore very little, were always barefoot, and many could not afford to go to school. But in the summer of 2007, Apoorva and Adarsha began to think that taking clothes to help the children was simply not enough. They wanted to come up with a bigger and better long-term plan.

In their own words

A famous ancient Chinese proverb says, "Give a man a fish and he will eat for a day. Teach a man to fish and he will eat for a lifetime."

Adarsha and Apoorva wanted to help the local farmers in India make more money from the crops they grew.

An inspired solution

Adarsha had a brilliant idea. Their father was concerned about the way that **fossil fuels**, such as coal, oil, and petrol, harmed the environment. These fuels are burned to make energy, and release harmful gases into the air.

Adarsha, Apoorva, and their father had been experimenting with "**greener**" forms of energy that did not harm the environment. They had been growing a plant called jatropha, which could be used as fuel on their own farm. Adarsha wondered if the villagers in India could grow jatropha on a large scale. They could sell it as fuel.

Jatropha plants can be used instead of diesel in cars.

Inspiring others to get involved

Adarsha and Apoorva realized that this was a huge project to get off the ground. They knew they would have to work hard to make their idea a reality. Apoorva took on the job of getting to know the villagers and convincing them that the plan was a good one. Meanwhile, Adarsha set about gaining the involvement of two big companies. One was a business that supplied **biofuel** plant seedlings and turned the grown plants into fuel. The other was an organization that worked with local farmers, trying to get them out of **poverty**.

Oil from jatropha seeds is used to make biofuel.

Kids who made a difference

In 1994, P.B.K.L. Agyirey-Kwakye was 14 years old, living in Ghana. He realized that local people were cutting down too many trees for firewood. The surrounding forest was disappearing and, without shade, they would no longer be able to grow cocoa – their main source of money. He managed to inspire the local farmers to plant Eucalyptus trees. These grow on dry soil and go from seedlings to the size of telephone poles in three years. They were great for firewood, shading cocoa crops, and could also be sold to builders for timber, to make more money.

To learn more about Apoorva and Adarsha's project, visit their website at www.projectjatropha.com.

Inspiring people around the world

Adarsha had won the California State Spelling competition. He used his prize of US$650 to buy enough jatropha seedlings to get the project going. Workers took the seedlings to farmers and showed them how to grow the plants. Project Jatropha was up and running! But Adarsha and Apoorva soon realized that they would need thousands of dollars to spread the idea.

Apoorva and Adarsha used their enthusiasm to inspire other people to get involved. A schoolfriend in the United States, Callie Roberts, joined the team to help raise money. An American company called Sirona Cares gave money to the project. An advertising company gave them a free computer program, which helped Adarsha and Apoorva to advertise their project and ask people for support.

Callie, Apoorva, and Adarsha have inspired people to help them because of their energy and hard work.

Reaching out

In 2009, Adarsha and Apoorva won an Action for Nature Eco-Heroes Award. But they didn't stop there. With Callie, they continued to reach out to school pupils, business people, and other groups in both India and the United States. They inspired people to give thousands of dollars to Project Jatropha. Callie has said, "Wherever we are there's an opportunity." About the future, she has commented, "I think if we can reach one individual, a team, a school, a community and beyond, our **momentum** will lead to great things."

In their own words

Apoorva Rangan, Adarsha Shivakumar, and Callie Roberts of Project Jatropha inspire others with this message: "If we do not lead by example, we are destined to be followers."

Adarsha and Apoorva have given talks about their work, and have won many awards.

25

Adora Lily Svitak: inspiring others to love learning

Adora Lily Svitak looks like an ordinary teenager from Seattle, Washington, USA. What she enjoys most in the world is school. But she isn't a pupil, she is the teacher! Adora has loved reading and writing since she was a very young age. She has made it her mission to inspire other young people to love books and learning too. She has become famous throughout the United States and all over the world.

Adora Lily Svitak comes from the city of Seattle, Washington, USA.

Early learning

Adora was born in 1997. When she and her older sister, Adrianna, were babies, they seemed to be very curious and clever. Their parents decided to start teaching them schoolwork early, at home. The children learned very quickly. Adora could read and write simple words by the age of two and a half. Her enjoyment of reading inspired a love of writing, and by the age of four she was starting to write short stories. However, as she turned five, her handwriting was too slow to keep up with her ideas. How could she write faster?

Adora read her first chapter books at just three and a half.

Top tips

Here are some hints on how to be a good writer:
- The more you read, the better you will write.
- Choose short things to write to begin with. Try poems, short stories, or entries in a diary, rather than aiming for a whole book.
- If you write speech, read it aloud to make sure it sounds real.

Technology helps

Adora's parents gave her an old laptop computer. Adora quickly worked out how to use "learn to type" programs, so her writing began to flow. By the age of six, she could type out 60 words per minute on the computer, rather than writing out her stories slowly by hand.

Adora makes good use of spellcheckers and online dictionaries.

By the age of seven, Adora had written over 300 short stories and was reading two books a day. A local television news company heard about her work and interviewed her on their programme. Adora was so inspiring that the producers of a famous national television programme, *Good Morning America*, asked her to appear on their show, too. She wrote a story live on air.

A book of her own

Adora dreamed of seeing her work in print, so she started sending off a collection of short stories, with tips for young writers, to **publishing companies**. But most people didn't even read it. They just assumed that her work would not be good enough because she was a child. But Adora did not give up. Eventually she found a publisher who agreed to print her work as a book called *Flying Fingers*.

Kids who made a difference

Children who are exceptionally gifted at something are called **prodigies**. Wolfgang Amadeus Mozart was a musical prodigy who lived over 200 years ago in Austria. He composed his first piece of classical music when he was just four. By the age of six, he was travelling around Europe giving concert performances. Mozart composed an entire **opera** when he was twelve. He has inspired countless other musicians.

Adora the teacher

Adora knew many children were not like her and didn't know how much fun learning could be. They didn't understand that gaining knowledge, skills, and ideas would help them in the future. Adora also realized that many adults didn't think children were capable of very much. They didn't help kids explore the world and their own abilities as they should. Adora decided to inspire both children and adults to change their attitudes.

When Adora was 10, her family converted the basement of their home into a television studio. She began teaching children, adults, and teachers by video link. Adora also travelled to more than 300 schools and classrooms worldwide, including China, Hong Kong, Vietnam, and the UK, spreading her message and her passion for learning. She believes all children should have an education, and so raises money for UNICEF and Save the Children.

Adora has taught at schools all over the world.

Inspiring adults

By the time she was 14, Adora was speaking at adult **conferences**, explaining to audiences how they can help children to love learning. She is the youngest person ever to receive an important prize called the NEA Foundation Award for Outstanding Service to Public Education. Most importantly, she has reached out to children worldwide and inspired thousands to read, write, and love learning. In 2010 and 2011, Adora organized her own conference, attended by over 1,000 young people.

Kids who made a difference

Christopher Paolini (shown here) was born in 1983 in Southern California, USA. When he was 15, he wrote a fantasy novel about dragons, elves, and dwarves called *Eragon*. It became a bestseller all over the world and was made into a film.

Craig Kielburger: working for children's rights

In 1995 in Canada, 12-year-old Craig Kielburger was flipping through his local newspaper in search of cartoons. He was struck by a story about a courageous Pakistani boy his age called Iqbal Masih. Iqbal had spent his childhood in slavery.

Craig Kielburger grew up near the city of Toronto, in Ontario, Canada.

N

ATLANTIC OCEAN

C A N A D A

ONTARIO

Montreal

0   500 miles
0   500 kilometres

U N I T E D
S T A T E S

Toronto

New York

Iqbal's story

Iqbal Masih was born in 1982 into a poor family in Pakistan. When Iqbal was four, he was sold as a **slave** to a moneylender. He worked with other enslaved children in a carpet-weaving business in terrible conditions. Aged 10, he escaped and joined an organization working to free child slaves like him, but was killed aged 12 by those who wanted to stop his good work.

Iqbal Masih freed over 3,000 child slaves and made speeches against child labour around the world.

Uniting for action

Craig was so moved by Iqbal's story that he took the newspaper article to school. He talked eleven friends into forming an **action group** to find out and **protest** about child labour. They called themselves the Twelve Twelve-Year-Olds, though they later changed this to Free the Children. What could they do to help?

Kids who made a difference

Om Prakash Gurjar was born in Rajasthan, India in 1992. He worked as a slave on a farm from the age of five and was often beaten. When he was eight, an organization freed him and he was able to go to school. Om Prakash has stood up for other poor children and campaigned against child labour. He has spoken to international leaders and won the International Children's Peace Prize.

33

A fact-finding mission

Craig wanted to know the facts and decided he needed to see child labourers for himself. In December 1995, Craig travelled to South Asia in the company of Alam Rahman, a 25-year-old family friend. He visited children working in terrible conditions in Bangkok, Kolkata, Karachi, and other cities. He made a film he could show people when he returned home.

Inspiring world leaders

During his trip to India, Craig learned that the Canadian prime minister was also in the country. Craig arranged a meeting of television and newspaper reporters. He announced that the prime minister should be trying to end child labour. After this, the prime minister met with Craig. Craig inspired him to discuss child labour with the president of Pakistan and the prime minister of India.

This is Craig, aged 13, talking about child labour at a news conference in Ottowa, Canada.

Spreading the word

Back in Canada, Craig and his schoolmates signed **petitions** and contacted world leaders, companies, and news corporations to protest about child labour. They gave speeches and presentations and inspired thousands of young people to raise money to help. Money came through donations, garage sales, car washes, cake sales, and sponsored events (where people donate money to charity if you complete an activity such as a race).

Within two years, Free the Children had inspired the use of a "Rugmark" label in Germany to mark carpets made without slave labour. A group of American sports goods manufacturers stopped buying footballs stitched by Pakistani child workers. Free the Children had raised enough funds to help open a rescue centre in Pakistan for kids who had escaped slavery.

Top tips

A petition is a great way for a group of people to show the strength of their opinion and influence decisions. If you would like to organize a petition to support a good cause:

- decide who to address your petition to
- write clearly at the start what you want them to do
- make numbered lines for names and addresses, so it is easy to see how many people have signed
- set up a petition on the internet, so more people can see it and sign it.

Inspiring young people

Next, Craig and Free the Children established "Friendship Schools", linking schools in North America and Europe with schools in poorer countries around the world. The young people involved brought about life-changing results. One school in Sierra Leone, where many children had been forced to fight as soldiers, received donations of books, pens, textbooks, and clothes.

As Free the Children grew, Craig travelled the globe. He met with world leaders, receiving awards and appearing on television shows to inspire others to raise money and get involved.

Changing lives

By 2004, Craig was 22. Free the Children had become an enormous international organization. They introduced a project called Adopt a Village. This employed staff in poorer countries to work with local communities on whatever projects they needed. These were often setting up schools, water wells, clinics, and business schemes to help reduce poverty. All this was paid for by young people, families, and businesses in other countries who were inspired by Free the Children to raise funds.

Craig (right) and his brother, Marc, appeared on the *Oprah Winfrey Show* on TV several times.

Free the Children needs young people all over the world to raise money.

In their own words

Brennan Wong is a Canadian boy who began fundraising for Free the Children at the age of eight. He says, "Halfway across the world, children don't get [birthday] presents . . . My 10th birthday last year was my most memorable so far. I realized that I could turn ordinary birthday parties into something meaningful by asking friends and relatives to donate to Free the Children instead of bringing gifts."

New ideas

In 2008, Craig and his brother Marc founded a new organization called Me to We. This was set up to support the work of Free the Children. Me to We organizes trips for young people and families who want to get involved with Free the Children projects overseas. It also has an online shop, where shoppers can support people in poorer countries by buying products made by them. When someone buys a book, a book is also given to a child in a poorer country.

Since 2007, Craig and Marc have held "We Day" for young people in Canada, to inspire fundraising for Free the Children.

Onward and upward

Craig and Free the Children have won countless awards. These include the 2006 World Children's Prize for the Rights of the Child, also known as the Children's Nobel Prize. The organization is now the largest ever network of children helping other children. It has inspired hundreds of thousands of young people to assist those in need, in 45 countries. They have no plans to stop any time soon.

Kids who made a difference

Fatema Begum grew up as one of nine children in a tin-roof shack in Bangladesh. From the age of seven, she worked in dreadful conditions in a match factory. As a teenager, Fatema paid for herself to go to school. She now works as a teacher at a centre for children who work in factories. Fatema inspires the kids to learn and achieve better futures.

Former child labourers make their beds at a rescue home in India run by Free the Children.

You can make a difference

None of the young people whose stories are told here set out to be role models. But that is what they have become. No one can fail to be inspired by their achievements. Each of the young people has achieved great things by following their hearts and their talents. The lesson for all of us is don't be afraid to be true to yourself.

Be inspired!

It doesn't matter how young you are, don't ever think you cannot do something. Start with a small goal, then set yourself another, and another. Ask other people, such as your family and friends, to help you. If you have a dream to achieve something, go for it. Let these stories of wonderful kids inspire you.

American Josh Shipp was brought up in foster care. He is now a successful author and television presenter. Based on his own experience of growing up, Josh gives motivational talks to young people to inspire them to achieve great things, too.

Kids who made a difference

Tavi Gevinson from Chicago, USA, began a fashion **blog** when she was just 11. Tavi's comments on fashion in her blog were so sharp and professional that she attracted thousands of readers. By the age of 14, top designers were regularly inviting her to fashion shows and asking her to write about their designs. Tavi now runs her own online magazine for teenagers.

In their own words

Talia Leman, who set up RandomKid says, "I have learned that anyone is someone. I allow myself to think big, and then I take all the small steps to get there, one after the other, never stopping. When I hit an obstacle, I see it as a wrong-way sign and head a new way."

Tavi has described herself as a "tiny dork that sits inside all day wearing awkward jackets and pretty hats."

Making a difference map

Arctic Ocean

N

Craig Kielburger (pages 32–39) lived in Toronto, Ontario when he was inspired to set up Free the Children.

NORTH AMERICA

Adora Lily Svitak (pages 26–31) teaches and writes from her home in Seattle, Washington, USA.

Apoorva Rangan and **Adarsha Shivakumar** (pages 20–25) live in Oakland, California.

Sam Levin (page 7) started an organic garden at his school in Massachusetts, USA.

Talia Leman (page 4) set up RandomKid from her home in Iowa, USA.

Abby Enck (pages 8–13) sold lemonade to help hospital patients in Chicago, Illinois, USA.

Atlantic Ocean

SOUTH AMERICA

Pacific Ocean

0   3000 miles

0   3000 kilometres

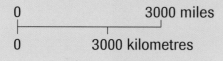

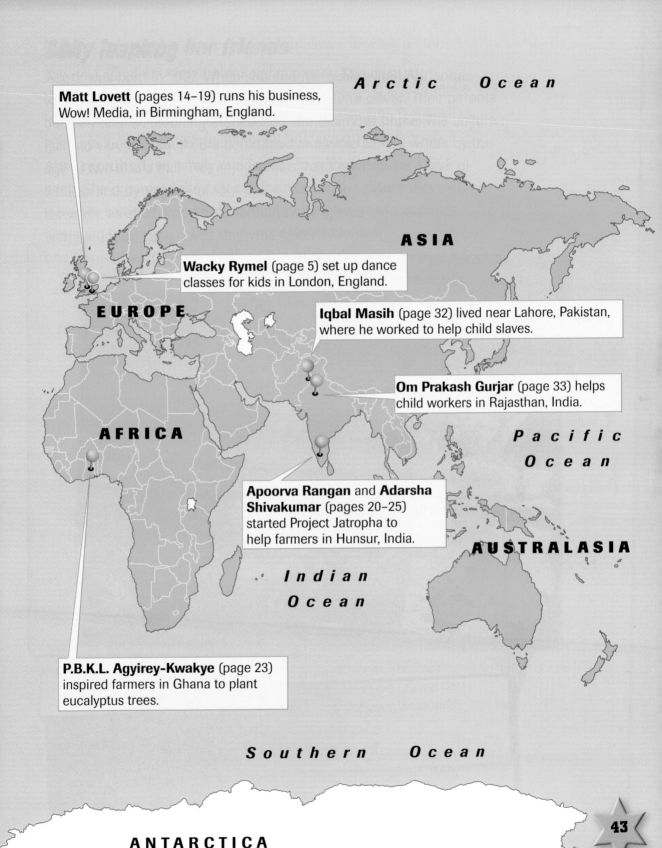

Arctic Ocean

Matt Lovett (pages 14–19) runs his business, Wow! Media, in Birmingham, England.

ASIA

Wacky Rymel (page 5) set up dance classes for kids in London, England.

Iqbal Masih (page 32) lived near Lahore, Pakistan, where he worked to help child slaves.

EUROPE

Om Prakash Gurjar (page 33) helps child workers in Rajasthan, India.

AFRICA

Pacific Ocean

Apoorva Rangan and **Adarsha Shivakumar** (pages 20–25) started Project Jatropha to help farmers in Hunsur, India.

AUSTRALASIA

Indian Ocean

P.B.K.L. Agyirey-Kwakye (page 23) inspired farmers in Ghana to plant eucalyptus trees.

Southern Ocean

ANTARCTICA

Tips on making a difference

Do you want to make a difference and inspire others to do the same? One way to do this is by volunteering. Volunteering means giving some of your time and energy to help good causes. Being a volunteer is a great way to make the world a better place and maybe even inspire others to help as well. It can give you the chance to meet new friends, learn new skills, and have fun!

How can I start volunteering?

You may already have a good cause in mind that you would like to help, such as a local animal shelter or litter-pick-up project. If you need to find a good cause that appeals to you, there are different websites that can help. Organizations such as www.do-it.org.uk or www.charitychoice. co.uk allow you to search charities by topic area.

Starting your own project

If you can't find the right project, you might want to start your own. This can be a big job, so don't be afraid to ask for help! Learn as much as you can about the problem you want to solve. Is there anyone else working towards the same goals, either in your community or elsewhere? You might be able to learn from them. Look at www.randomkid.org. This organization, set up by 13-year-old Talia Leman in 2008, loans money to inspired young people to help them jumpstart their own volunteer projects.

Can I volunteer with other young people?

A great way to get involved as a volunteer is to join the girl guides or boy scouts. As a member of one of these groups, you will get to help a wide variety of good causes, and will meet new people, too. Look at these websites for more information:

* www.girlguiding.org.uk
* www.scouts.org.uk

Talk with a trusted adult

Many of the young people featured in this book had help and support from their parents and other trusted adults. You should discuss your idea with a parent, teacher, or club leader. An adult will help you stay safe. They can provide advice and check to see that any organization you want to help is worthy of your time and effort.

Involve others

Working together leads to success – there is strength in numbers! When starting a new project, try to find people who share your goals and will help you. You may be surprised at how eager your family, friends, and schoolmates are to lend a hand.

Glossary

action group group of people who have banded together to achieve an aim

apprentice person who is learning a trade from a skilled employer

biofuel fuel made from plants

blog if someone keeps a blog, they record their thoughts on a website on a regular basis

brainstorm group discussion to come up with new ideas

cause worthwhile aim or organization

cerebral palsy medical condition in which someone's muscles don't work as they should. This is often because their brain has been damaged before or at birth.

conference large gathering of people to present information and discuss ideas

coordination ability to move different parts of the body smoothly and at the same time

determination commitment to work hard at something and not give up

donate give as a gift, to help a person or project

empower enable someone to do something

entrepreneur someone who risks their money to start up a new business idea

environment natural world around us

fossil fuel fuel found naturally in the earth, such as coal, oil, or natural gas

green energy form of energy that is not harmful to the environment, such as energy made from the wind and the waves

inspirational something that stirs people to get up and take action

momentum forward movement

opera theatre production in which performers tell a story by singing to classical music

organic plants that have been grown in natural conditions without the use of chemicals

petition protest that collects as many people's signatures as possible in support of a cause

poverty being extremely poor

prodigy someone who is remarkably gifted at something from a very young age

profit amount of money someone makes from selling something, after taking away all expenses

protest expression of disapproval in words or actions

publishing company business that makes books

recruit employ someone specially to do a task

role model person other people look up to as a good example

slave person who works for another without pay or rights

underprivileged not having as many opportunities or as good a standard of living as most people

Find out more

Books

Anne Frank (Great Lives), Ann Kramer (QED, 2007)

Inspirational Lives (series) (Wayland, 2011)

Political Activism: How You Can Make a Difference (Take Action), Heather E. Schwartz (Snap Books, 2009)

Social Justice: How You Can Make a Difference (Take Action), Lynn Bogen Sanders (Snap Books, 2009)

Websites

www.changemakers.com/stories/unexpected-success-for-the-randomkid-solving-real
Visit this website for the full story of Talia Leman, inspirational founder of RandomKid.

www.ecokids.ca/pub/eco_info/topics/kids/index.cfm
Go to this site to read the stories of some amazing kids from Canada and their world-changing projects – including Craig Kielburger and his organization, Free the Children.

www.inspiringyoungpeople.co.uk
This is an online magazine which showcases teenagers and young adults all over the world who are doing inspiring things.

2012.youthsporttrust.org/inspiring-young-people/index.html
Visit the Youth Sport Trust's site to find out about the work of the inspiring Young Ambassadors for sport in Britain.

www.charity-commission.gov.uk
The Charity Commission regulates charities in the UK. Visit their website to find information on charities and their projects, and to learn about setting up your own.

www.freethechildren.org
Learn more about the organization set up by Craig Kielburger.

Index